Not Another Tea Party

Written by
Mark Shulman

Illustrated by
Vincent Nguyen

Sterling Publishing Co., Inc.

New York

For Miriam and Leah, who are definitely not Hilary. –M.S.

For Jack and Deborah Nix. –V.N.

Special thanks to Frances and the original Hilary, without whom this book (and Frances) would not have been possible.

Library of Congress Cataloging-in-Publication Data Available

10   9   8   7   6   5   4   3   2   1

Published by Sterling Publishing Co., Inc.
387 Park Avenue South, New York, NY 10016
Text © 2006 by Mark Shulman
Illustrations © 2006 by Vincent Nguyen
Designed by Joe Bartos

O•MF

Created at Oomf, Inc.
www.Oomf.com

Distributed in Canada by Sterling Publishing
C/o Canadian Manda Group, 165 Dufferin Street,
Toronto, Ontario, Canada M6K 3H6
Distributed in the United Kingdom by GMC Distribution Services,
Castle Place, 166 High Street, Lewes, East Sussex, England BN7 1XU
Distributed in Australia by Capricorn Link (Australia) Pty. Ltd.
P.O. Box 704, Windsor, NSW 2756, Australia

Printed in China

Sterling ISBN-13: 978-1-4027-3304-8
          ISBN-10: 1-4027-3304-6

For information about custom editions, special sales, premium and
corporate purchases, please contact Sterling Special Sales
Department at 800-805-5489 or specialsales@sterlingpub.com.

Hilary was having another tea party.

She always wrote four invitations. One for Stuffy Bear.
One for Mister Big Arms. One for herself, since she loved to
get invitations. And one for the fourth seat.

The fourth seat was usually empty.

Sometimes a cousin or two would come over, but they never stayed long.

They just could not follow all the rules for a Hilary tea party.

Hilary hugged Stuffy Bear tight. "We don't need anyone else, Stuffy. Just us three."

One especially long Sunday, Hilary got a great Hilary idea.
This idea required very careful planning, and extra politeness,
because it involved Mom *and* a fresh batch of cookies.

Of course, Hilary got her way.

The great Hilary idea began with a handmade invitation of the finest construction paper. Hilary left it on the bus stop bench.

Then she left a trail of cookies down the path, up the steps, and straight through Hilary's red front door.

Hilary settled down to wait, but she didn't have to wait long.
First she heard the clump, clump, clump of slow footsteps.
Then the creak of the bedroom door. Then she saw a big
green head.

A big green head?

Standing at the door, partway in and partway out, was a giant chameleon. In its mouth was Hilary's invitation.

"A chameleon, hmmm?" said Hilary, who did not appreciate lizards, large or small. "I suppose you can join our tea party. It's very exclusive."

Hilary did not know what to think. This wasn't the guest she was hoping for, but she gave him one of her warmest greetings.

"You can *not* sit there!" she screeched. "That's where Mister Big Arms always sits."

Chameleons naturally have terrible hearing, so this one paid little attention to Hilary. Mister Big Arms soon found himself with a whole new view.

"You'll be all right once you learn to follow instructions,"
said Hilary, after pouring the world's fanciest pretend tea.
"Put on these ears. Those are the rules."

The chameleon did not wear the ears. "I suppose it's just
bad breeding," decided Hilary, and she let it go. Soon enough,
Hilary got another terrific Hilary idea.

"If you won't put on the ears, put on a show," said Hilary. "Chameleons change color, right? Let's see that."

This time the chameleon was happy to oblige.

"Do another! And another!" Hilary clapped at the parade of colors and patterns. For the grand finale, the chameleon turned pink.

"Hey, you can't turn pink!" said Hilary. "Pink is *my* color!"

Things quickly slid from bad to worse. The chameleon, who was still hungry, reached for a cookie. *Zap!* went his long, sticky tongue. *Zing!* went the cookies.

"Eek!" went Hilary, right into the chameleon's face.
"*Never* touch the cookies with your tongue!"

And so, having had enough of a Hilary tea party,
the chameleon snatched up the rest of the snacks and
took Mister Big Arms away with him. Soon they vanished
out the front door.

Hilary was too surprised to get up from her seat.

"You don't have to come back," she called out, "but bring back those cookies!"

The room got very quiet. Hilary didn't take her eyes off the front door. Finally, she turned slowly to Stuffy Bear.

"I guess it's just you and me now."

Stuffy turned his head and spoke for the first time.

"I'm sorry," he said. "It's just no fun. You're too bossy."

Then Hilary's stuffed animal pushed back from the table and climbed off his chair.

"Come find me when you can play nicely," said Stuffy Bear.

Then he walked past Hilary and out the door.

Hilary sat alone with all her friends.

After a time, the sound of laughter and lively chatter
drifted through the front door.

Hilary tiptoed and Hilary peeked. And what did Hilary find?

She found all her friends having another tea party.
And there was even a place set for Hilary.